A FUNNY THING HAPPENED TO... SI SIDEBOTTOM

P. Crumble and Dean Rankine

A Koala book by Scholastic Australia

Koala Books
An imprint of
Scholastic Australia Pty Limited
PO Box 579 Gosford NSW 2250
ABN 11 000 614 577
www.scholastic.com.au

Part of the Scholastic Group
Sydney • Auckland • New York • Toronto • London • Mexico City
• New Delhi • Hong Kong • Buenos Aires • Puerto Rico

Published by Scholastic Australia in 2018
Text copyright © P. Crumble 2018
Illustrations copyright © Dean Rankine 2018
The moral right of the author and illustrator have been asserted.

A catalogue record for this
book is available from the
National Library of Australia

NATIONAL
LIBRARY
OF AUSTRALIA

ISBN: 978-1-74381-038-5

Printed in Australia by Griffin Press.

Scholastic Australia's policy, in association with Griffin Press, is to
use papers that are renewable and made efficiently from wood grown in responsibly
managed forests, so as to minimise its environmental footprint.

18 19 20 21 22 / 1

Welcome to my **CRAZY** day!

Not only do you get to join me on a bunch of **TOTALLY FUNNY ADVENTURES**, but guess what? **YOU** get to choose what happens to me next. When you see the words, '**Then a FUNNY THING happened . . .**' that's your cue to choose where I head next or to follow the page number to the next **super-embarrassing** part of my day.

SO LET'S GO!

Simon Sidebottom

Then a FUNNY THING happened . . .

Pg 5. Welcome to
Simon's Wacky World

My name is Simon Sidebottom and I'm having a very bad day. Okay, okay, let's just get this out of the way. Yes really, my last name is Sidebottom. **S–I–D–E–B–O–T–T–O–M**. Go on. Have a good chuckle. Make a joke. Maybe draw a little picture of what you think I look like. Actually, here, I drew one earlier to save you time . . .

I've spent my whole life fake laughing at the lame jokes that everyone comes up with. I can totally reassure you that my rump is in the rear. My bum is behind me. My **backside** is on the **back side**.

So no, despite what you may think, the source of my bad day is not my last name!

Today is the last day of school holidays. And instead of enjoying my final hours of freedom, my mum wants to take me shopping. For **new school shoes!** In fact, there she is right now yelling at me . . .

'SIMON SIDEBOTTOM

get in the car **NOW!** We're going shopping for new school shoes.'

WIGGLE
WIGGLE

SIMON
SIDEBOTTOM!

Mum comes charging towards me with my baby sister—otherwise known as **SNOT FACE**—tucked under her arm like a gross slimy football. The look on Mum's face is serious. She means business.

'**SIMON!** Why aren't you in the car yet?' Mum says. 'I need help cleaning up your sister. She's got a RUNNY NOSE and has CHUCKED UP a little bit.'

Yikes! I don't have a choice, do I? I have to do as Mum says, right?

Then a FUNNY THING happened . . .

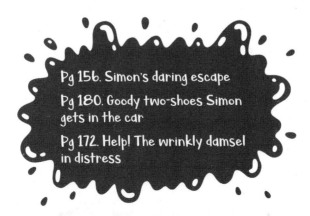

Pg 156. Simon's daring escape

Pg 180. Goody two-shoes Simon gets in the car

Pg 172. Help! The wrinkly damsel in distress

'But, **MUM**, I don't want to go to the **emergency room**,' I moan through Mr Fluffykins' furry belly.

Mr Fluffykins spies Mrs Nesbitt and promptly abandons my face and jumps straight into her arms.

'Just get me a few bandaids and I'll be fine,' I say bravely.

Ten minutes and a packet of FAIRY PRINCESS BANDAIDS later, my face is back in one piece.

8

'OKAY, YOUNG MAN,' says

Mum. 'You look well enough to go school-shoes shopping.'

SLICE   SLICE

SHRED

Then a FUNNY THING happened . . .

Pg 18. Crazy car chaos

9

My first thought is, maybe the **HUGE BEAST** will simply walk around our car. Boy, am I **wrong**.

The elephant takes a sniff at the car. Then, using its **MASSIVE HEAD**, starts pushing the car along the road like a toy. It then sticks its trunk under, flips the car on its roof and spins it around like a top. Bored with that, Tiny uses the car to **SCRATCH HIS BUTT** and then moves on.

The crowd **CHEERS** as if this was part of the circus act!

Then a FUNNY THING happened . . .

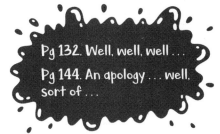

Pg 132. Well, well, well . . .

Pg 144. An apology . . . well, sort of . . .

The **ENORMOUS** bird belongs to **Bobo the Happy Clown**. Bobo is taking part in the circus parade a few streets away and is unaware that his 'pet' is on the loose.

Bobo's **BIG BIRD** decides to take Mr Fluffykins back as a gift  to Bobo.

The bird circles the parade a few times before releasing a **furious** Mr Fluffykins midair. The **HOWLING** cat drops down into the parade.

BINK

Then a **FUNNY THING** happened . . .

Pg 158. Mr Fluffykins drops in for a visit

Pg 150. Bullseye!

Yes, this is pretty much one of the most **humiliating experiences** of my life. Covered in **SNOT** from head to toe and scaring the general public. Oh and it's the final day of holidays. Yup, this day is going well. **NOT.**

And that's when I feel the first drop of rain. In all the commotion, I didn't notice the dark storm clouds overhead. There is a **HUGE CLAP** of thunder and the downpour starts. The **SNOT** that's covering us slides from our bodies and gurgles down the drain.

Now that the **GREEN SLIME** has cleared, I can see the grim look on Mum's face.

'We're getting on the next bus and going to the shops,' Mum says firmly. Boy, she is not a happy camper!

Then a FUNNY THING happened . . .

Pg 108. Bus, bus, where are you taking us?

15

So here we are. Three **DRIPPING SLIME MONSTERS**, standing on the footpath with people running away from us.

A voice from behind us calls out,

'AWESOME COSTUMES, DUDES!'

I turn around to see a middle-aged man in a **tight, yellow one-piece outfit** with a **RED LIGHTNING BOLT** on the front. The outfit is completed with a green towel around his shoulders like a cape. He is a **WALKING FREAK SHOW**.

'Do you like my **CAPTAIN INCREDIBLE** costume?'
he asks. 'Your **SWAMP CREATURE** outfits are
totally **AMAZING!** You look like you're heading
to the Comic Book Convention. **FOLLOW me**, it's just
around the corner.'

Then a **FUNNY THING** happened . . .

Pg 106. Welcome to nerd city

Resigned to my fate I get into the car. **SNOT FACE** is strapped into her car seat and covered in **GROSSNESS**. My baby sister always has **DROOL**, **BOOGERS** or **VOMIT** on her (and often all three at the same time).

As Mum drives down the street, I start cleaning **SNOT FACE**. It's a pointless task because her nose, mouth or backside are always producing some **VILE SUBSTANCE**.

It isn't fair that my final day of holidays is going to be spent shopping for boring school shoes. I slump back into the car seat with a **DEEEEEEEP SIIIIIIIIGGGGGH**. There are so many **great** ways I could be spending my final day of holidays . . .

Then a FUNNY THING happened . . .

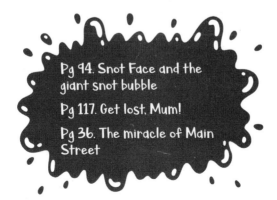

Pg 94. Snot Face and the giant snot bubble

Pg 117. Get lost, Mum!

Pg 36. The miracle of Main Street

'Oh good boy, Simon,' Mrs Nesbitt sings out with glee. 'You've saved Mr Fluffykins! Look, he seems to **LIKE YOU!**'

My **HYSTERICAL SOBBING** is muffled by Mr Fluffykins' fat furry belly. I can't see **A THING**, but I know I have to get this cat off my head—**fast!** Using my hands and feet, I feel my way back down to the bottom of the tree. Now the **greedy guts** is snacking on my ear!

Someone get this cat OFF MY HEAD!

'Come here, you **cheeky devil**,' gurgles Mrs Nesbitt. 'Come to Mamma for kisses.'

I'm not really sure whether Mrs Nesbitt is talking to me or Mr Fluffykins. With a growl, Mr Fluffykins unwraps himself from my head and **Leaps** into Mrs Nesbitt's arms. Mum starts fussing over Mrs Nesbitt. **No really, I'm okay, Mum! THANKS FOR ASKING!** So I take the opportunity to sneak back to our yard.

'SIMON! WHERE DO YOU THINK YOU'RE GOING?'

 yells Mum.

Then a FUNNY THING happened . . .

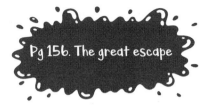

Pg 156. The great escape

SPRING

CRACK...

CRAACK...

CRAAAA

24

25

Branches splinter as I crash through the tree like a **human chainsaw**. I can just see my neighbour's cat, MR FLUFFYKINS, watching it all from the top. Did he just FLIP HIS MIDDLE CLAW at me?

My life flashes before me and wow, it's **totally boring!** I close my eyes and clench my teeth, waiting for the bone-shattering impact of my body hitting the earth. But it doesn't come. My jeans have snagged on a branch, giving me an EYE-BULGING WEDGIE. **OUCH!** It may have been less painful to SPLATTER on the ground.

Then a FUNNY THING happened . . .

Pg 30. Mr Fluffykins makes a soft landing

Pg 88. In the event of a wedgie, dial 000

I am **HIGH-FIVING** myself and **desperately**
hoping that someone in the circus crowd has filmed
my **seriously spectacular** jump.
Footage like that would go **VIRAL** and I would be
TOTALLY FAMOUS!
As I cruise down the street dreaming of **fame** and
fortune, a bike **SKIDS** in front of me. And
SHOWERS ME with gravel. **Thanks
a lot!**

'**NICE TRICK, KID.** I was doing jumps just like that
before I could walk,' the stranger says with a laugh.

28

The stranger speeds off while doing a
HANDSTAND on the HANDLEBAR.

TA-DA!

Then a FUNNY THING happened . . .

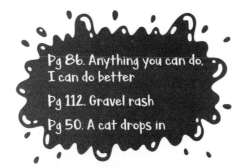

Pg 86. Anything you can do,
I can do better

Pg 112. Gravel rash

Pg 50. A cat drops in

I look up as Mr Fluffykins makes a **loud wailing sound**. He swishes his tail back and forth. And then he's in the air. In **SLOW MOTION**, I see the cat dive towards me, legs outstretched and claws extended.

You know how they say that cats ALWAYS land on their feet? Well, I can **definitely confirm** this is true. Mr Fluffykins makes a perfect landing. A perfect landing

ON MY FACE.

The tubby feline is now firmly wrapped around my head.

Then a FUNNY THING happened . . .

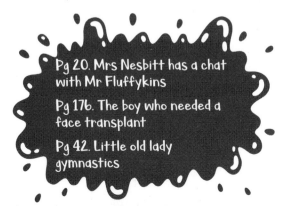

Pg 20. Mrs Nesbitt has a chat with Mr Fluffykins

Pg 176. The boy who needed a face transplant

Pg 42. Little old lady gymnastics

'You'll see . . . how I help you **PUSH THE CAR** to the side of the road and call the road service for you.' Bobo the Happy Clown gives us a **SMILE.**
WOW, that **CERTAINLY** is **NOT** how I was expecting things to go down.

Bobo **whistleS** ♫♪ to **TINY THE ELEPHANT** and soon the car is pushed safely out of the path of the circus parade.

Within fifteen minutes we are back on the road.

Then a FUNNY THING happened . . .

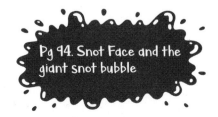

Pg 94. Snot Face and the giant snot bubble

It is not

a **terrific**

time for Mr

Fluffykins' NERVOUS

BLADDER to kick in.

He decides **right now**

to go kitty tinkle. Lucky **SNOT**

FACE's habit of FLICKING BOOGERS at me has

given me **amazing reflexes. Wobbling**, I dodge

the tinkle waterfall and manage not to fall out of the tree.

'**Come on, puss-puss**,' I gently call out.
'Come to your **FRIEND** Simon.' The cat **OBVIOUSLY**
doesn't speak my language.

Then I hear it. A **FEROCIOUS**
swooshing noise that is getting CLOSER and
CLOSER. I look up in time to see a **MASSIVE**
BIRD pluck Mr Fluffykins out of the tree.

Then a **FUNNY THING** happened . . .

Pg 76. Simon's getting carried away

Pg 12. A gift for Bobo

Mum drives down the road and turns onto Main Street.

I'm still **plotting** ways of how I can manage to get

my **FINAL DAY OF FREEDOM** back. But it

looks **HOPELESS**. I'm trapped and there is

no way out. I watch as **SNOT FACE** plays

BOOGER BINGO on the back of the car seat. My

little sister is **so gross**.

Then the **MIRACLE HAPPENS**. The car starts to

splutter. And cough. And then it rolls to a **stop**. We are out

of petrol.

I see Mum's eyes **WIDEN** as she looks in the

rear-view mirror. **Looming** behind us is a **CIRCUS**

PARADE and we're **right in the way**.

I peer through the back window and see a **HUGE**

ELEPHANT heading towards us.

36

'EVERYONE OUT!' cries Mum.

I grab **SNOT FACE** out of her seat and join Mum at the side of the road.

Then a FUNNY THING happened . . .

Pg 10. Tiny the Elephant plays toy cars

Pg 168. Mum versus Bobo the Happy Clown

We all let out a **SHOCKED GASP** as Mrs Nesbitt launches herself out of the tree. 🌲 The gasp may be because she's using her dressing-gown as a parachute. But actually it's probably because the old lady is now dressed in **onLy her undies!**

Clasping the parachute in one hand and the cat in the other, Mrs Nesbitt starts *drifting slowly downwards.*

Mr Fluffykins has other plans though. He **squirms** and **wriggles** and **nibbles** until he is finally **free** of Mrs

38

Nesbitt's grasp. The cat looks pleased with himself for a millisecond until he starts ROCKETING TOWARDS EARTH. Fortunately, my head stops puss-cat from going splat . . .

Then a FUNNY THING happened . . .

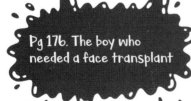

Pg 176. The boy who needed a face transplant

I can't believe it! Somehow, I'm in **ONE PIECE**. It's a **MIRACLE!** A quick check of my pants confirms that the smell is coming from the elephant and not me.  And the best part? My bike has made it over the parade as well! **BONUS POINTS** for the fact that Mum is trapped on the other side.

SUCCESS! Maybe I'm going to be able to enjoy my final day of holidays without shopping for school shoes . . .

Then a **FUNNY THING** happened . . .

Pg 140. What's a V.A.M?

Pg 28. No-one is cooler than Simon Sidebottom. Except . . .

Seeing her DARLING CAT in **MORTAL DANGER** must have kick-started old Mrs Nesbitt's heart. Seeing me in danger was obviously **NOT ENOUGH** to get her moving! She **jumps up** and grabs hold of the nearest branch. And then, **LIKE A GYMNAST**, she

SPIN

swings herself **branch by branch** ever **HIGHER**.

She is soon balancing beside her beloved Mr Fluffykins. It's a

magnificent display of **ACROBATICS** and

OLD-LADY UNDERPANTS.

Mrs Nesbitt skilfully unhooks Mr Fluffykins' claws and scoops

up the cat. Then, using her dressing-gown as a parachute, she

LEAPS off the branch.

Then a FUNNY THING happened . . .

Pg 128. Mrs Nesbitt floats away

Pg 38. Mr Fluffykins wriggles free

Pg 148. Meanwhile, back on the ground . . .

We try to wipe the **GREEN SLIMY SNOT** from our bodies, but it's hopeless. The more we try, the more **PANIC** it sends through the crowd.

'Look, that **SLIME MONSTER** is doing a war dance,' cries one alarmed bystander. He's pointing at Mum, who is hopping around, trying to shake snot off her leg.

Within minutes there are helicopters buzzing overhead and police vans pulling up. Could this day get any **WORSE?**

Then a net lands on top of us.

Then a FUNNY THING happened . .

Pg 146. Oops we've made a mistake

AAH!
WEE-WOO
WEE-WOO
SIRENS!
DON'T MOVE!
POLICE!
ACTION
FREEZE!
POLICE
SWAT!
ATTENTION!

The bus continues to **HURTLE** down strange streets.
I make my way up to the driver to ask him where we are
headed. He refuses to answer and points to a sign.

> ### DO NOT TALK
> ### TO THE DRIVER
> ### WHILE THE BUS
> ### IS IN MOTION.

'That's really **not very helpful**,' I tell the driver.
He just taps the sign and looks ahead.

As I make my way back to Mum and **SNOT FACE**,
the bus comes to a **SCREECHING
HALT**. I am CATAPULTED straight into the
strange old lady's lap.

The driver turns to us with a **SPOOKY SMILE** and announces, **'LAST STOP.'** And then he gives a **creepy Laugh.**

We step off the bus because we have no choice.

Then a FUNNY THING happened . . .

Pg 52. Super-creepy old lady

Pg 118. A familiar wrinkly face

I look back towards the ambulance and I'm surprised to see Mum and **SNOT FACE** grimly holding on to the side of the stretcher. **Great (read: NOT great),** they've decided to come along for the ride.

We gather pace as we hit the dip leading towards Main Street. **WE HAVE TO CONTROL THE STRETCHER SOMEHOW!** We throw our weight to the left, then to the right. We navigate through a circus parade and down a freeway. We then go through several shopping centres before the stretcher finally comes to rest.

'Mum, you can open your eyes now,' I say.

When Mum finally opens her eyes, a **big, sinister smile** comes across her face.

'Well, this is just perfect.' She laughs.

48

Then a **FUNNY THING** happened . . .

Pg 110. I saw the sign

Pg 96. The bus stop

They say that life is a series of **RANDOM EVENTS**. Well, I've certainly got that covered.

I am about to chase after the handstand-on-handlebar stranger when I hear wailing. It's coming from above. It's **somewhat familiar** and has a **cat-like quality**. It sounds like our neighbour's cat, Mr Fluffykins.

Squinting into the sun, I can make out a **LARGE BIRD** carrying Mr Fluffykins.

I watch as the cat squirms his way free of the bird and starts to fall. The **wailing** gets **ANGRIER** and **LOUDER**. And closer. And he's about to **Land on my face!**

50

I open my mouth to scream but all I hear is a relieved purr from Mr Fluffykins. He's clearly happy that my face has saved him. I, on the other hand, **am NOT!**

What's also clear is that My Fluffykins isn't going to leave my face **WITHOUT A FIGHT**. I wobble back to my house wearing Mr Fluffykins around my head.

Then a FUNNY THING happened . . .

Pg 176. The boy who needed a face transplant

We have **NO IDEA** where we are. The bony-handed old lady seems to be waiting for us. She's looking **super creepy**.

She starts gesturing for us to follow. '**I know what you seek** . . .' she hisses. She then **DISAPPEARS** around the corner.

Mum and I look at each other. Should we follow the creepy old lady? **SNOT FACE** doesn't seem fussed one way or the other. My little sister inserts another finger into her **NOSTRIL**.

I shrug my shoulders and follow the old lady. Then a FUNNY THING happened . . .

Pg 167. An introduction

Pg 74. Surprise, surprise!

In the distance a circus parade continues down Main Street. Mr Fluffykins is actually in the **PERFECT SPOT** for a **great view** of the parade! But I guess he's too busy concentrating on not falling a spectacularly long way out of a tree.🌲

What we don't know is that Tiny the Elephant ate **A LOT** of beans for his breakfast. The huge elephant is enjoying the parade when his bowels start to **RUMBLE**. Tears come to his eyes as he tries to hold in the **BUBBLING TOXIC GAS**. 'Maybe I can just let a little bit out . . .' Tiny thinks.

BAAARP.

That's exactly the moment when things really get away from him.

BAAAAAAAAAAAARP!

And the moment when the smell hits us in Mrs Nesbitt's front yard. At first the breeze is gentle. A **STINKY, WARM DRAFT** swaying the branches of the tree ever so softly. Then comes the **noise**. I've never heard a noise this **TERRIFYING**. It **BOOMS** across the town and we're hit with a hot, farty gust that shakes the tree.

Being a fat ball of fluff with claws, Mr Fluffykins is blown about by the hot blast. We see the shaken cat hanging on by one claw.

BBAAAAAAAA

Then a **FUNNY THING** happened . . .

56

Pg 30. Mr Fluffykins makes a soft landing

Pg 42. Mrs Nesbitt leaps into action

With sirens **BLARING**, the ambulance lurches off down the street. Unfortunately, the paramedics are so busy **LAUGHING** at me that they forget to properly close the ambulance doors.

Before Mum can stop it, my stretcher **rolls out the doors**. The ambulance is headed one way and I am flat on my back on the stretcher heading the **other way**.

Then a FUNNY THING happened . . .

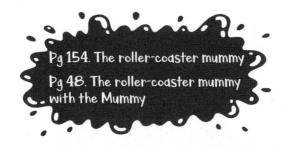

Pg 154. The roller-coaster mummy

Pg 48. The roller-coaster mummy with the Mummy

I take off **like a rocket** and I'm pretty much hitting **WARP SPEED** by the end of the street. Just as I make a skidding right turn into Main Street, MY HEART SINKS. The road is blocked. **The circus has come to town!**

The road is clogged with CREEPY CLOWNS, **farty**

elephants and many bearded ladies (or is it bearded elephants and farty ladies?). **THERE IS NO WAY THROUGH!**

But wait, just ahead there is a ramp . . . In a millisecond I'm **AIRBORNE**, heading straight over the parade . . .

Then a FUNNY THING happened . . .

Pg 164. Tiny the Elephant lends a hand (or trunk!)

Pg 134. Bobo the Happy Clown turns nasty

The **GREEN SLIME** is everywhere. Nothing has escaped. Including Mum and me. It's **gross multiplied by disgusting**. We come to a skidding halt.

Stumbling onto the footpath, we stand there dazed and dripping. That's when we hear the panicked screams.

'SLIME MONSTERS . . . RUNNNNNNNN!'

Then a **FUNNY THING** happened . . .

Pg 44. Put your slimy hands in the air

Pg 16. Saved by a comic book nerd

Pg 14. Rain, rain saves the day

TERROR!

WOW! It's not every day you look to the sky and see a flying pussycat 🐱. Then we hear the commotion a few streets away. Why is the **ground rumbling**? What is that **pounding sound** that is getting closer and closer?

All good questions that are quickly answered as Tiny the Elephant **BURSTS** out of the bushes. And there's Mr Fluffykins holding on with grim determination! The elephant is heading directly towards us!

My years of watching *When animals attack silly people* television shows kick in. I stand directly in front of the beast, put my hand up and shout at the top of my lungs,

'STOOOOOPPP!'

The elephant, of course, **does not** stop. I even see Mr Fluffykins put his paw over his eyes.

Impact in three, two, one . . .

Then a FUNNY THING happened . . .

Pg 121. It's happening all over again . . .

Fifteen minutes later a white van pulls up beside us. Mum is **positively grinning** at this stage. It's the type of grin that can ONLY MEAN TROUBLE.

The side of the van SLIDES OPEN slowly. There is an old man sitting on a stool and behind him shelves covered with curtains.

The old man pulls back the curtains. And there on those shelves are **at least a hundred pairs of school shoes**.

POINT
POINT

'Hello, Simon,' croaks the old man. 'Welcome to **PINCH AND BLISTER'S MOBILE SHOE-FITTING SERVICE**. We've got **hours** of shoe-fitting fun ahead of us . . .'

THE END

After a short ride, we arrive at the back of a dusty old building. We climb a set of rickety stairs and I follow Emma inside. In the gloom, I can make out an old man hunched over a table.

'Simon Sidebottom, meet my grandad, **Enzo Blister**. He runs the famous **PINCH AND BLISTER** shoe shop.'

Enzo whirls around and looks at my tattered sneakers. His eyes gleam. 'Hello, Simon, I've been waiting for you. Your mum has you booked in for some shiny new school shoes. We should be all done in around five hours . . .'

NOOOOOOOOO!!!!

Word of our plight has obviously got around. Just as we think **no-one** will help, Mum is tapped on the shoulder by a man. A man wearing a GAS MASK.

'Mmmmm dbbb fft ki?' the man asks.
'WHAT?' Mum says.

MMMMM DBBB FFT KI???'
repeats the man.

'I CAN'T HEAR YOU THROUGH THE GAS MASK,' Mum yells. 'WE NEED HELP.'

Frustrated, the man pulls of his gas mask and yells back,

'DO YOU WANT TO USE MY PHONE?'

The poor chap then faints from the smell.

Mum pulls the phone from the unconscious man's hand and makes a call.

She hangs up and tucks the phone back into the man's pocket. What is that SMIRK on her face all about?

Then a FUNNY THING happened . . .

Pg 64. The white van

SNOT FACE's stench is **so powerful** that it wafts clear over to the other side of town. Exactly where a circus parade is making its way slowly down the street.

BIG GLORIA THE GORILLA is a hulking ape with a heart of gold and super-sensitive nose. She sniffs the air and off she **charges**. Whatever that stink is on the other side of town, she wants part of it! **Nothing** will stand in her way.

RARRR!

In the distance we see buildings crumbling and cars being smooshed as **BIG GLORIA** charges towards us. She comes to a shuddering stop in front of us.

BIG GLORIA sniffs my little sister adoringly and then whips her out of Mum's arms. Cradling **SNOT FACE** like a baby, **BIG GLORIA** charges back towards the circus parade.

Like a flash, Mum jumps back in the car and screams, **'Get in!'** And then we are chasing **BIG GLORIA.**

Then a FUNNY THING happened . . .

Pg 114. Follow that ape!

BOBO THE HAPPY CLOWN struggles to regain control of the unicycle. I'm standing on his shoulders and wobbling about like crazy. It's not looking good for either of us. We both see the speedbump at the same time. BOBO tries to swerve around it, but we **hit it with force**. And just like that, I am back in the sky and TUMBLING DOWN. I close my eyes . . . I am going to be **tasting the road** at any moment . . .

BANG!

Wait a minute—NOTHING IS BROKEN!
I'm not smooshed anywhere. My legs and arms feel normal. I open my eyes—**I'M NOT ON THE ROAD.** I've landed on the back of **TINY THE ELEPHANT!** And he is quite **startled** by my surprise visit. His massive trunk swings over his head and flicks me off his back **like a flea.**

Then a FUNNY THING happened . . .

Pg 78. Stinky Simon

Pg 40. What goes up must come down

My jaw drops. I CAN'T BELIEVE IT.
After all day of trying to get out of shoe shopping,
right smack in front of me is . . . **heaven!**
DAVE'S DAZZLINGLY SUPER-
AWESOME AMUSEMENT
AND WATERSLIDE
PARK!

Score! I run in to spend the **best final day of holidays ever!**

THE END

DAVE'S

S.A.A&W.P

RIDES

YAY

The bird **SWOOPS** down
past me. Mr Fluffykins
is just within my reach.
Well, his tail is anyway. I
grab onto that **fat, furry,
sausage-like tail** and I'm
lifted off the branch.

   Mr Fluffykins is **NOT** impressed
by me dangling off his tail. He starts
swiping wildly with his sharp little
claws. Unfortunately, he is not a good aim and he ends
up poking the giant bird **IN THE BUTT**. In response, the
giant bird lets go of a **giant bird-poop.** The nugget
is on target for a direct hit to my head! My reaction is to let
go and cover my face.

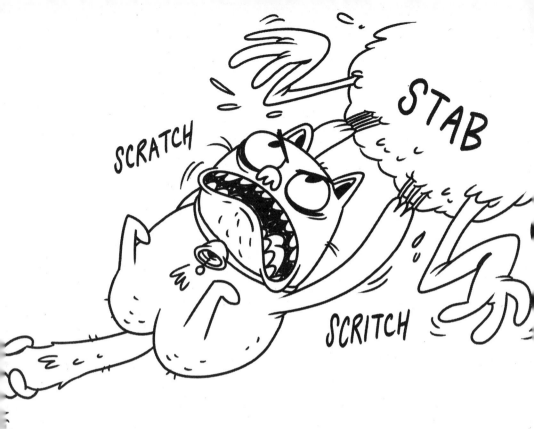

Then a **FUNNY THING** happened . . .

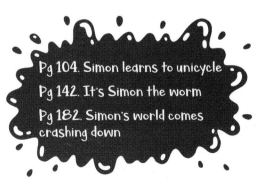

Pg 104. Simon learns to unicycle

Pg 142. It's Simon the worm

Pg 182. Simon's world comes crashing down

The landing is soft. In fact, it's **too soft**. And **too STINKY!** Tiny the Elephant is taking part in the circus parade and Tiny has eaten a lot of beans for breakfast. MAJOR YUCK!

Mum hauls me out of the pile of **elephant poop** and cleans me off with **baby wipes** and **spit**. I am marched back to the car.

Then a **FUNNY THING** happened . . .

Pg 18. Crazy car chaos

I can **taste** the freedom.

I can **feel the wind** in my hair.

I can hear my mum **bellowing** at me.

I can see **SNOT FACE**'s Baby Go Potty dolly LYING DIRECTLY IN FRONT OF ME...

ARRRRGH, TOO LATE!

I swerve and hit the brakes. The bike **skids** and **bucks**. My **BUM** flies up off the bike, and then my WHOLE BODY is in the air. With a great **plonk**, I land on the soft grass in the yard next door before finally sliding to a stop.

I can hear Mum's **HUFFING AND PUFFING** nearby . . .

Then a **FUNNY THING** happened . . .

Pg 172. Mrs Nesbitt calls for help

Pg 184. I've got grass stains all over my sidebottom

It takes the biker gang a moment to **fully grasp** what has just happened. A kid has hijacked their leader's bike and is escaping down the road with his SCREAMING MUM and baby sister in the sidecar. Now **that's embarrassing!**

All those years of playing video games are paying off. Riding a motorcycle is simple and **boy** does it go **FAST!** I **ZOOM** down streets and across town. We are back in familiar territory and not that far from home.

I can hear the gang behind me though. They are catching up fast. There is too much weight with Mum and **SNOT FACE** in the sidecar. I round a corner and come to a screeching halt. '**Get out**,' I yell at my family.

With Mum and **SNOT FACE** safe, I gun the bike and head towards Main Street. It's blocked by a circus parade. I have no other choice but to try to **jump over the parade**.

The jump starts off fine and smooth. Then, I am **in the air** and no longer on the motorbike.

WOOSH

Then a FUNNY THING happened . . .

Pg 104. Simon learns to unicycle

The gang leader whips off his helmet. He's **bushy-bearded** and **tattooed**. I swear, even his BEARD has TATTOOS.

His deep, gruff voice booms, 'Looks **Like you're in a LOT** of trouble . . .'

At that moment the **stench** from SNOT FACE enters his nostrils.

With **WATERING EYES** the gang leader squeaks, **'Let's get outta here.'** The gang screeches off, scared by a baby's full nappy.

It's a shame they leave early because they miss out on **SNOT FACE**'s other favourite trick.

SNOT FACE lets out a **HUMONGOUS SNEEZE**. The amount of **SNOT** that flies from her nose is astounding. We're covered from head to toe in **DRIPPING GREEN SLIME**. But at least the slime blocks the stench that's seeping out of **SNOT FACE**! I guess there's always a bright side . . .

We are pretty much the **grossest people** in the city.

Then a **FUNNY THING** happened . . .

Pg 16. Saved by a comic book nerd

The stranger on the bike is cocky, but they haven't seen my

mad bike skills. I TEAR OFF after them and cut

in front while standing on the bike seat and doing a front-wheel

stand.

'CHALLENGE ACCEPTED,' the stranger cries out.

The stranger **soars** down a steep dip in the road and then

does **THREE FULL SOMERSAULTS** before landing

safely.

'**Top that, kid,**' the stranger yells.

Never one to be shown up, I plan to unleash my

SIMON SIDEBOTTOM SIX SOMERSAULT

SHOWCASE. I pedal towards the dip and reach maximum

speed. And then my foot slips off the pedal and I crash down

heavily onto the bike frame. I feel a pain only a boy can know.

I plant my feet on the ground to slow myself down. But it isn't

working.

To my credit I stay on my bike. But by the time I come to a standstill, my sneakers are SMOKING and my toes are POKING THROUGH.

'That was really lame,' the stranger says with a **smirk**.

Then a FUNNY THING happened . . .

Pg 188. A helping hand (or foot)

The commotion has drawn **quite a crowd** of nosy neighbours and onlookers. My jeans are snagged good and proper. I can't wriggle my way free and every movement just adds to the **MEGA WEDGIE PAIN**. Great, I'm going to be rescued by the fire department and it's going to be

ALL OVER THE NEWS.

I'll **never** LIVE THIS DOWN.

It strikes me as odd that **MR FLUFFYKINS** is rescued **first**, but soon enough I'm slung over the shoulder of a fireman and heading down the ladder. I can see Mum waiting **IMPATIENTLY**, ready to whisk me off to go **shoe shopping**.

'Simon, stop mucking about and get in the car . . .'

Then a
FUNNY THING
happened . . .

Pg 117. Get lost, Mum!

Pg 152. Simon the celebrity

89

Mum and **SNOT FACE** are with me in the back of the ambulance, while the **giggling paramedics** sit upfront. I'm looking directly at my little sister and see her nostril twitch. I've been her older brother for a couple of years, so I know this tiny movement is a **SMALL BUT SIGNIFICANT** signal of what is about to happen . . .

The nostril twitch turns into a nostril flare. The nostril flare releases a trickle of green. The trickle of green turns into a river. And as the river is just about to hit her mouth, **SNOT FACE**'s head flies back, mouth wide open . . .

'ΛΛΛΛHHH CHOOOO!'

The sound of the sneeze ricochets around the ambulance. And the **green slime hits** . . .

90

Then a **FUNNY THING** happened . . .

Pg 60. Attack of the slime monsters

'Come on, we'd better chase after Mrs Nesbitt!' I cry.

Genius! It's the perfect excuse to delay going shoe shopping.

Mum, **SNOT FACE** and I jump in the car. Through the car window we catch sight of Mrs Nesbitt. Mr Fluffykins is still **FIRMLY ATTACHED** to her hand.

She is drifting downwards and skims over a birthday party. Mrs Nesbitt's aim is perfect. As she **gLides over the top**

of a **BOUNCY** castle, she lets go of the dressing-gown parachute. It's a lovely, soft landing. Except she didn't factor in the **BOUNCINESS** of the castle.

After an epic **HIGH BOUNCE**, Mrs Nesbitt ends up landing **HEAD-FIRST** in the birthday cake.

92

'She's safe,' Mum says with a smile. 'Now that we're

FINALLY in the car we can go **shoe shopping** . . .'

Then a **FUNNY THING** happened . . .

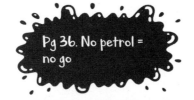

Pg 36. No petrol =
no go

Sharing the back seat of the car with my little sister is always a gross-out experience. **SNOT FACE** hasn't stopped mining for **GREEN NUGGETS** the entire time. But **miraculously**, her fingers finally leave her nostrils. She gives me a **SINISTER SMILE** and her face screws up like she has sucked on a lemon.

'AHHH CHOOOOOOO!'

From her nose **SNOT FACE** blows the biggest **SNOT BUBBLE** in the history of **SNOT BUBBLES**. It just gets bigger and bigger until finally—

'BOOM!'

Then a FUNNY THING happened . . .

Pg 123. Snot Face slimes the windscreen

Pg 190. There's no place like home

Pg 60. Attack of the slime monsters

96

I think Mum has completely **LOST THE PLOT.**

After our daring stretcher ride, she starts to **Laugh hysterically**. She laughs then sobs. Sobs then laughs. I use my bandages to wipe up her tears. **SNOT FACE** just sits there with her finger up her nose.

Once Mum has settled her nerves, we quickly determine that we have **NO IDEA** where we are. There is, however, a nearby bus stop. We might as well get on a bus.

Then a FUNNY THING happened . . .

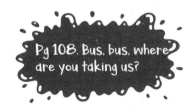

Pg 108. Bus, bus, where are you taking us?

The smell from **SNOT FACE**'s nappy is **terrifying**. We think that escaping the car will help. But the **TOXIC STINK CLOUD** is attached to my little sister and surrounding us.

People walking past us start covering their noses and gagging. Mum tries asking a few people for **HELP**, but they either run away screaming or pass out from the stench.

SPLERP!

Then a **FUNNY THING** happened . . .

Pg 70. Going ape over Snot Face
Pg 67. Gas-mask man

Mum **frantically** wipes at the front window, trying to clear the **SNOT**. She scrapes a small **PEEP-HOLE** through the **GOO** and edges the car to the side of the road.

'We need to go back home to clean up.' She sighs. 'There's **NO AMOUNT** of baby wipes **in the world** that will deal with this mess.'

What both Mum and I fail to notice is a **SECOND SNOT BUBBLE** forming in my little sister's right nostril. By the time we get to our street, the **bubble** is at **MAXIMUM CAPACITY.**

POP!

SNOT FACE

BLOWS.

BLINDED, Mum tugs sharply on the steering wheel. We veer into Mrs Nesbitt's yard! Mum **slams on the brakes**. Through the **SNOT HAZE** I can see Mrs Nesbitt standing next to the huge tree in her garden. And we're HEADING STRAIGHT FOR HER!

Mum and I **SCREAM** as the car skids past Mrs Nesbitt

and softly nudges the tree. 🌲

As we jump out of the car, we hear Mrs Nesbitt's cat high up

in the tree. Mr Fluffykins is hanging on by a paw.

ONE

BY

ONE

we see his claws lose grip . . . I clamber up the tree, but there is

so little time . . .

Then a **FUNNY THING** happened . . .

Pg 30. Mr Fluffykins
makes a soft landing

I FLY **QUITE** a distance **through the air**. The ground seems like a long way away. I spin and spiral and like to think I'm **PRETTY GRACEFUL**. But I can see I'm heading downwards **FAST.**

One final flip and I land **hard. VERY HARD.** Right on the shoulders of Bobo the Happy Clown, who is part of the passing circus parade. The problem is that BOBO IS RIDING A UNICYCLE . . .

Then a **FUNNY THING** happened . . .

Pg 134. Bobo the Happy Clown turns nasty

Pg 72. Meet Tiny the Elephant.

With nothing to lose, we decide to follow the nerd into the convention. Inside there are all kinds of **WEIRDOS** in costumes. And then I catch a glimpse of Mum, **SNOT FACE** and me in a mirror. **Um, yep**. We fit right in with this lot.

After we win the '**best dressed**' competition—tickets to Dave's Dazzlingly Super-Awesome Amusement and Waterslide Park—Mum herds us into a bathroom to clean up.

We are soon back on the street looking like humans.

Then a FUNNY THING happened . . .

Pg 118. A familiar wrinkly face

Pg 108. Bus, bus, where are you taking us?

A bus soon pulls up and we get on and settle back into our seats. The only other passenger besides Mum, **SNOT FACE** and me, is an old lady with large bony hands. She keeps **Looking at me** and **cackling**. Do I still have **SNOT** on my face?

The bus heads down a series of streets and the surroundings start to look less and less familiar.

'Mum, do you know exactly where this bus is taking us?'

Then a FUNNY THING happened . . .

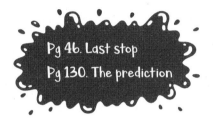

Pg 46. Last stop

Pg 130. The prediction

I look up and through my bandages I see the sign . . .
it couldn't be???

PINCH AND BLISTER SHOES.

NOOOOOO!

THE END

Never one to be outdone, I try the **one-wheel-handstand-on-the-handlebar** trick.

This is easier than it looks, I think **SMUGLY** as I haul myself into the handstand. Or maybe I'm just **RIDICULOUSLY SUPER TALENTED.**

But of course, I've overlooked a couple of minor details.

Firstly, when you're upside down in a handstand, it's **really difficult** to steer a bike.

Secondly, exactly how do you **STOP** a bike when you're doing a **HANDSTAND** on the handlebars?

The bike gathers speed and soon I'm **wobbling** out of control back towards the circus parade. And then a hole in the road answers my second question. The bike stops with A JERK and I cartwheel through the air. I am going to **face plant** directly on the road.

Then a FUNNY THING happened . . .

Pg 78. Stinky Simon

Mum and I follow Big Gloria the Gorilla back across town through the **DESTRUCTION** she has caused.

The gorilla rejoins the circus parade and is now holding **SNOT FACE** high up in the air like she's presenting her baby to the world!

Spying a school friend in the crowd, I run over, borrow his bike and **PEDAL FURIOUSLY** towards the trapeze that the Amazing Acrobatic Bearded Ladies have set up. I **expertly bunny hop** the bike onto the safety

TEE-HE!

net and bounce up towards the trapeze. Letting go of the bike, I hook my leg over the bar. And that's the easy part! From this upside-down lookout, I see the bike sail clear across the parade. Dangling by my legs, I swing towards Big Gloria and **SNOT FACE. SNOT FACE** reaches up with her **SNOT-COVERED HANDS** and I snatch her out of Big Gloria's **goriLLa grip.** I toss **SNOT FACE** into Mum's waiting arms.

Unfortunately, **SNOT FACE** has managed to **completely SLIME MY HANDS**. They're so **GOOEY** that when I try to pull myself upright on the trapeze I slip . . .

Then a **FUNNY THING** happened . . .

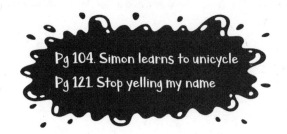

Pg 104. Simon learns to unicycle

Pg 121. Stop yelling my name

So **SNOT FACE** and I are in the back of the car and Mum is driving us to the shops. My little sister has been **mining** for **GREEN NUGGETS** the entire time. The whole finger-up-the-nose-and-wiping-it-on-the-back-of-Mum's-head routine has been distracting Mum. We are on a freeway heading in the wrong direction! Five boogers later, we're clear across the city.

BIG MISTAKE. We're lost and in a bad part of town.

'**ROLL up the windows**,' Mum yells.

Then a **FUNNY THING** happened . . .

Pg 136. Snot Face makes a bad smell

Pg 160. The car becomes suddenly lighter

Pg 132. Well, well, well . . .

We're **scratching our heads** wondering what to do next when a beaten-up old car **TOOTS ITS HORN**. The car pulls over towards us and stops. The window slowly rolls down.

'**What are you folks doing all the way out here?**' the driver croaks.

HANG ON, I know that voice. 'It's Mrs Nesbitt from next door!' I say in surprise.

'Oh thank goodness, Mrs Nesbitt.' Mum sighs. 'Can you give us a lift home?'

It's a long trip home with Mrs Nesbitt travelling at **old-lady speed.** I reckon I could get out and push the car quicker. I also can't help noticing that Mrs Nesbitt has been out and about in her dressing-gown.

GOOD FOR HER, I think. If I could get away with it, I would do the same.

Hours later we arrive back home. It's getting late and I'm super tired, but guess what? **I'VE ACTUALLY WON!** No school-shoes shopping for Simon Sidebottom!

Mrs Nesbitt invites us in for afternoon tea.

PUTT
PUTT
PUTT
PUTT

Then a FUNNY THING happened . . .

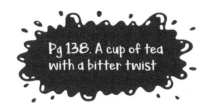

Pg 138. A cup of tea with a bitter twist

BEEP,

BEEP,

BEEP!

The noise in my ears is **LOUD** and **PERSISTENT**.

120

I imagine myself as flat as a pancake and rescuers having to use some type of **LARGE EGG FLIP** to lift me off the road.

In the distance I can hear Mum **yelling**,

'SIMON. SIMON . . .'

I sit **bolt upright** in my bed. I am in ONE PIECE!
I was JUST DREAMING! And then I remember . . .
it's the last day of school holidays . . .

Then a FUNNY THING happened . . .

Pg 7. Final day of holidays

The giant snot bubble hanging out of **SNOT FACE**'s left nostril explodes. The noise from my little sister is like a **FIRECRACKER** going off. Followed by a **WET, GREEN, SLIMY SPRAY** that covers **everything**, including Mum and me.

'I can't see through the front window!' cries Mum.

Then a FUNNY THING happened . . .

Pg 100. Mum's crazy driving (or Mum's driving me crazy)

The gang leader's **DEEP, GRUFF VOICE BOOMS**, 'Looks like you're in a **Lot** of **trouble** . . .' He then whips off his helmet.

Mum's eyes widen. 'Nigel Nerdsly, is that you?'

Turns out that Mum and Nigel were in a high school BIRD WATCHING CLUB together. They haven't seen each other in YEARS and have a LOT of catching up to do.

'Let's go for iced tea and the gang can sort out the car,' says Nigel, clapping his hands with glee.

The hand clapping **STARTLES** several birds that have clearly been nesting in Nigel's beard. They **noisily squawk** and **flap** about his head before **SETTLING BACK IN**.

After **TWO LOOOOOOOONG HOURS** of hearing about YELLOW BELLIED SAP SUCKERS, we're **finally** back in the car and on our way.

Then a **FUNNY THING** happened . . .

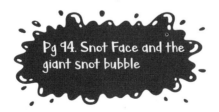

Pg 94. Snot Face and the giant snot bubble

Mrs Nesbitt's **wrinkly, underwear-clad body** is dangling from her dressing-gown parachute. She is holding the parachute with one hand and has a firm grip on Mr Fluffykins with the other.

The cat's **FURIOUS SWISHING TAIL** acts like a propeller and it starts to push the pair away from us. **Far, far away**. The last thing we can make out is Mr Fluffykins taking a nibble on Mrs Nesbitt's hand. He must be hungry . . .

Then a **FUNNY THING** happened . . .

Pg 158. Mr Fluffykins drops in on Tiny the Elephant

Pg 92. Follow that wrinkly old lady!

129

I turn to the **CACKLING BONY-HANDED OLD LADY** and ask where the bus is headed.

She hisses, '**I know where YOU'RE headed, YOUNG MAN. ABANDON ALL HOPE NOW . . .**'

Um, yep, **SUPER CREEPY**. Just as I thought. I shrug

my shoulders and turn back to Mum.

'**Last stop**,' the bus driver announces.

Then a **FUNNY THING** happened . . .

Pg 52. Super-creepy old lady

We hear the **ROAR** of the motorcycles before we see them. Well, honestly, at first I think it's **SNOT FACE** and her never-ending stream of **FARTS**. But then we see a trail of **exhaust smoke** in the distance.

Soon we're surrounded by **scary-Looking** bikes being ridden by **EVEN SCARIER-LOOKING** dudes and dudettes.

'WeLL, weLL, weLL, what do we have here?' the gang leader growls . . .

Then a **FUNNY THING** happened . . .

Pg 84. Scaredy-cat bikers

Pg 124. The reunion

Pg 162. We're being taken for a ride

Bobo the Happy Clown **REALLY** does not live up to his name. He is in fact **downright cranky** that I have crashed the circus parade. He obviously doesn't **APPRECIATE** my **perfect ten-point Landing** on his shoulders while he's riding a unicycle!

The crowd, however, thinks we are

BRILLIANT .

We **wobble** about and I put on **quite a show**. I don't think Bobo appreciates me **STANDING ON HIS HEAD** though. After the crowd stops cheering, Bobo whistles to Tiny the Elephant. In a **SWIFT MOVE**, the beast **snatches** me off Bobo's shoulders and I become trapped in his trunk.

SHOVE

Tiny then uses my **head** to CLEAN HIS EARS OUT.

'Who does this **grubby little child** belong to?' Bobo bellows.

From the crowd I hear Mum's angry voice. '**SIMON SIDEBOTTOM!** You march back to the car right now!'

Then a **FUNNY THING** happened . . .

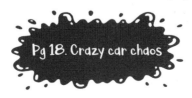

Pg 18. Crazy car chaos

So, Mum, **SNOT FACE** and I are

stranded.

That's not **TOO BAD**, is it? It's better

than going school-shoes shopping. Or is it?

SNOT FACE makes a little

GRUNTING SOUND. Her face

goes **red** and is all SCREWED UP.

And then she **giggles**. That's when the

smell hits. The **EYE-WATERING**

STINK is OVERPOWERING.

'That is **not normal!**' a panicked

Mum screams.

Then a **FUNNY THING** happened . . .

Pg 98. Why are people so unkind?

Pg 132. Motorcycle mania

I practically **skip** into Mrs Nesbitt's house. By the time we finish our afternoon tea it will be way **TOO LATE TO GO SHOPPING FOR SCHOOL SHOES**. Plus, Mrs Nesbitt makes the most **awesome** vanilla slices. **SCORE!**

We're ushered into Mrs Nesbitt's living room. There is an old lady sitting in an armchair. Mrs Nesbitt introduces the lady as her sister, Tootsie Pinch.

As I help myself to **several** vanilla slices (maybe at least ten!), both Mum and Mrs Pinch start laughing. Must be a **funny old-lady joke**. Or someone **accidently farted**.

'Simon. Come over here,' Mum calls out. 'Mrs Pinch has something to tell you.'

I gulp down another half of a vanilla slice and wander over.

Mrs Pinch takes my hand. 'Simon, I know you've been disappointed because you haven't been able to get the school shoes you need,' coos Mrs Pinch. 'Don't you worry though. I **OWN** Pinch and Blister Shoes and just for you we'll keep the store **open**. You'll have your brand-new school shoes even if it takes all night.'

NOOOOOOO!

THE END

I coast down the street **congratulating myself** on my **SICK SKILLS**. Seriously, who has ever pulled off a feat of cruising over a circus parade? **Me, that's who!**

I am a legend.

I AM THE COOLEST GUY AROUND,

I AM . . . BEING FOLLOWED BY A CAR.

Not just any car, but the mum-mobile driven by a **VERY ANGRY MUM**.

chug chug

Mum must have sprinted back to the house, strapped in **SNOT FACE** in the baby seat and driven around (or through!) the circus. She sure is **determined** to get me into a NEW PAIR OF SCHOOL SHOES!

Mum swerves the car and skids to a halt in front of me. I know when I'm beaten. Without a word I climb in.

Then a FUNNY THING happened . . .

Pg 117. Get lost, Mum!

The **cat-claw-butt-poking** incident has made the bird **VERY ANGRY** and determined not to miss out on a big part of her dinner—**ME!** With a **DEAFENING SCREECH**, the bird swoops downwards and snags my foot with her beak. Mr Fluffykins and I are **carried away**.

Our destination is a nest at the top of a **MASSIVE TREE**. As soon as the bird drops us into the nest, the cat makes a **dash** down the tree. I can see Mr Fluffykins **HURTLING** back towards his home. **'Thanks a lot, buddy.'** I think.

I look around and can see eggs and **squawking baby birds** of the **GIANT** variety. Their beaks are open and they're **HUNGRY** . . .

'PEEP, PEEP, PEEP . . .'
BEEP, BEEP, BEEP . . .

Then a **FUNNY THING** happened . . .

Pg 122. It's happening all over again

143

I think Tiny the Elephant feels bad for wrecking our car.
He wanders back towards us, offering Mum a **SINGLE**
DAISY he has **daintily plucked** from the edge of
the road. Why couldn't he be so **gentle** when it came to
our car?

Tiny walks off, leaving behind a **STINKY**
ELEPHANT FART for us to chew on.

Then a **FUNNY THING** happened . . .

PLERP

Pg 136. Snot Face makes a bad smell

Mum, **SNOT FACE** and I are bundled into the back of a van and **whisked away**. When the van stops and the doors open, we are in a HUGE WAREHOUSE. **Bright spotlights shine down** on us and men in white coats scurry about.

'What type of alien monsters do you think they are?' whispers a white coat.

'The **REALLY GROSS TYPE**,' answers another geeky scientist.

That's when Mum **EXPLODES**. She has been through enough.

'**Listen here, nerds.** I'm just a mum taking my son shopping for school shoes. And my daughter seems to have a **SLIGHT SNIFFLE**.'

On cue more **GREEN STUFF** dribbles from **SNOT FACE**'s nose. And after all this, I **can't believe** that Mum is still insisting on taking me shopping!

After a proper hosing down, the science geeks are satisfied that our story checks out.

We're driven home and arrive just as our car is being unloaded from the back of a truck. It provides the perfect distraction . . .

Then a FUNNY THING happened . . .

Pg 156. Simon's daring escape

Way to go, Mrs Nesbitt! The lady is an **absolute Legend!** Not only has she CLIMBED A TREE in record time and saved her cat, she has used her **dressing-gown** as a **parachute** AND **landed safely** without breaking any brittle bones! What's more, she has DISTRACTED MUM long enough for me to make my escape.

I sneak back into my yard and jump on my bike . . .

SNEAK SNEAK

Then a FUNNY THING happened . . .

Pg 58. The circus comes to town

Float
Float
Float

I jump on my bike and track Bobo's bird from the ground.

Bobo's bird is a **DARN GOOD AIM** and he delivers the

bewildered cat straight into the clown's arms.

By the time I arrive at the circus parade, Bobo is

JUGGLING Mr Fluffykins along with a **pumpkin** and a

chainsaw!

Mum, **SNOT FACE** and Mrs Nesbitt pull up in the

car.

TOSS

SPIN

I have only **MOMENTS** to decide. I can still escape my **shoe-shopping nightmare**. But I would have to jump over the parade.

I PEDAL FURIOUSLY towards

the parade and up the ramp of a parked truck . . .

Then a FUNNY THING happened . . .

Pg 164. Tiny the Elephant lends a hand (or trunk!)

THROW

Mum is interrupted by a CAMERA CREW and a **pushy reporter** with a microphone. Terrific, the local news is already on the scene. I am going to be **'famous'**.

'So that looked REALLY BAD. **HOW painful** was your **wedgie?**' is the reporter's first question.

She quickly follows up with, 'So you didn't even manage to save the cat???'

152

I catch a glimpse of the live interview on a portable screen. Under my image sits the headline, 'Clumsy child rescued from tree'.

The footage of me being rescued by the firemen is quickly spreading across the internet. And people I know are watching it. And texting me.

My phone is going **crazy** . . .

BEEP, BEEP . . .

BEEP, BEEP . . .

BEEP, BEEP . . .

HA

HA

HA

HA

HA

Then a FUNNY THING happened . . .

Pg 122. It's happening all over again

'This isn't so bad,' I think as I **ROLL DOWN THE STREET** watching the clouds in the sky. Then the road dips away and I start going, **FASTER** and **FASTER**.

Just ahead at the next intersection I can see a crowd of people. There's a **circus parade** heading down Main Street. There is **NO WAY** of stopping the stretcher!

K-SCHWING

Thinking quickly, I **unwrap my head**. As I roll past a tree, I throw the bandages over a branch and swing across the parade. Magic! The stretcher heads into the parade, rolls UNDER AN ELEPHANT and narrowly misses **COLLIDING** with Bobo the Happy Clown. The stretcher emerges on the other side and I drop back down onto it.

Then a FUNNY THING happened . . .

Pg 140. The mum-mobile

It's **NOW** or **NEVER**. **What to do?** It comes down to three basic questions.

1. Do I want to spend my **final day of holidays** having my feet **painfully squeezed** into school shoes?

DEFINITELY NOT!

2. Would seeing my **feet being tortured** make Mum happy?

HMMM, NOT SURE ABOUT THAT.

3. Should I throw **CAUTION TO THE WIND** and live on the edge?

DEFINITELY.

DECISION MADE. Mum can move **quite quickly** for an oldie, but I reckon I can make it to the bike in time. With **ninja speed** and **agility**, I roll across the front yard, scoop up my helmet and leap onto my bike . . .

LEAP!

SUCCESS! I'm away and pedalling fast.

Then a FUNNY THING happened . . .

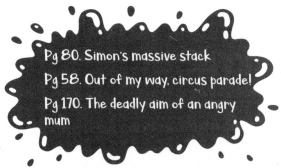

Pg 80. Simon's massive stack

Pg 58. Out of my way, circus parade!

Pg 170. The deadly aim of an angry mum

Tiny the Elephant is feeling **much better** after a little **GRUMBLY TUMMY** upset.

'The circus parade is going really well,' thinks Tiny. 'I'm sure no-one noticed me **CROP DUSTING*** my way down the street.'

What he doesn't expect is for a cat to land directly on his back.

With a '**MEOOOOW . . . POOOMPH . . .**' Mr Fluffykins has arrived!

The startled elephant lets out a **ROAR** and **ROCKETS** through the crowd. Mr Fluffykins holds on for **dear life** like a cowboy in a rodeo.

Then a FUNNY THING happened . . .

Pg 62. Simon makes a stand

*Crop dusting (noun): **PASSING GAS** in a stealthy manner, usually while walking through a crowd.

We cruise down the unfamiliar street full of **CRUMBLING HOUSES**. Mum spies a corner store that is still open. 'We can ask for directions in there and then get back to buying school shoes,' Mum says.

We are in the store for two minutes. Maybe three minutes tops. We emerge with directions in hand and find that the car looks a little different . . .

All the wheels have been **stolen** and the DOORS are **missing**! Seriously, WHO STEALS CAR DOORS?!

Then a FUNNY THING happened . . .

Pg 136. Snot Face makes a bad smell

Pg 118. A familiar wrinkly face

The gang leader insists that we **go for a ride**.

'Um thanks anyway, but it's a NICE DAY for a walk . . .' I say.

'**I wasn't asking** . . .' the gang leader barks.

As he loads Mum and my little sister into the sidecar of his motorbike, I see an **opportunity for escape**. But I have to do it WITHOUT HESITATION. I jump on the seat of the motorbike, gun the throttle and the bike and sidecar roar off. Mum's shrieks can be heard from miles away. SNOT FACE thinks it's way cool though as a string of GREEN SNOT flies out behind her.

SCREECH

Then a **FUNNY THING** happened . . .

Pg 82. Simon the biker

AH!

I am **KING OF THE WORLD** and sailing **gracefully** through the air like a **SUPERHERO.** Well, I was, for about three seconds. **BLAST!** I am not going to make it.

At this rate, I'm going to land **SMACK BANG** in the middle of the parade. In fact, I'm going to land on the **Largest** and **STINKIEST ELEPHANT** I have ever seen. From up here I can see that this beast has not stopped **POOPING** for the last two blocks.

WINK

I am coming in for landing . . . right on the elephant's **massive head**. I make eye contact with the beast and I swear he winks at me.

KAWOOSH

Just as my **BIKE HITS HIM,** **HE LIFTS HIS TRUNK.** Instead of falling on my face, the bike rolls down the trunk, then launches off the **UPTURNED TIP.** I'm back in the sky and **BRACING MYSELF FOR DISASTER . . .**

Then a **FUNNY THING** happened . . .

Pg 40. What goes up must come down

The super-creepy old lady **SHUFFLES** towards a dark, dusty old shopfront.

'Let me introduce myself,' the old lady croaks. 'My name is Tootsie Pinch and I know what you seek. I've owned this store for many decades and I know the look of a young man who is on the **last day** of his **SCHOOL HOLIDAYS** . . .'

With **WILD CACKLING** ringing in my ears, I look up to the shop window . . .

'PINCH and BLISTER Shoes!'
NOOOOOO! There is no escape.

THE END

167

Bobo the Happy Clown appears from behind the elephant and comes quickly **wobbling** towards us on a unicycle. He's **waving his hands** and **shouting angrily.** So much for 'happy'!

'What do you think you're doing?' shrieks Bobo. '**MOVE THAT CAR NOW!**'

'I can't,' says Mum. 'We're out of petrol.'

'Well, lady that's **not my problem**. I've got **JOY** to bring to this SAD LITTLE TOWN,' screams Bobo. 'Move that car OR ELSE . . .'

'**OR ELSE, what?**' Mum challenges.

'You'll see,' Bobo roars.

Then a FUNNY THING happened . . .

Pg 32. Mum finds out what 'or else, what' is

Pg 10. Tiny the Elephant plays toy cars

Glancing over my shoulder, I'm surprised to see Mum **red-faced** and **puffing**. She's giving chase LIKE AN OLYMPIC SPRINTER. Who knew that a **VERY ANGRY MUM** carrying a toddler could move that fast? I PUMP THE PEDALS HARDER and start to gain some distance. I even **stand up** on the pedals and do a **Little bum waggle** at her. Bad move, Simon. Very bad move.

FWOOOSH

In one swift movement, Mum flicks off a thong and **throws it like a boomerang**. The rubber shoe BOUNCES off the side of my head and the bike starts to

wobble out of control. The next thing I know I'm flying through the air . . .

Then a FUNNY THING happened . . .

Pg 78. Stinky Simon
Pg 26. Simon versus a tree

CHOK!

PEDAL
PEDAL

'**HELP!**' comes the old lady's shriek. It's Mrs Nesbitt from next door. '**WON'T SOMEONE COME AND HELP MEEEEEEEE?**' she croaks.

I can never resist helping a **damsel in distress**. Even one as **wrinkly** as old Mrs Nesbitt. Dressed in her ALARMINGLY SHORT dressing-gown, Mrs Nesbitt is pointing high up in the tree to her **precious cat**, Mr Fluffykins.

'Don't worry,' says Mum, suddenly standing behind me. 'Simon will climb the tree and rescue him. After that we've got school shoes to buy.' And she gives me her **STERNEST LOOK**.

173

Climbing a tree versus shopping for school shoes! **No contest.** I jump onto the tree and start clambering up with **MONKEY-LIKE SKILLS.**

Mr Fluffykins is **clinging unsteadily** onto the pointy top of the tree. He's a **HEFTY LUMP** of a cat and his weight is making the thin branch **droop.** As I climb **higher**, the branches become **skinnier** and soon I'm standing pretty much on twigs. Of course these will hold my weight, I reassure myself . . .

Then a FUNNY THING happened . . .

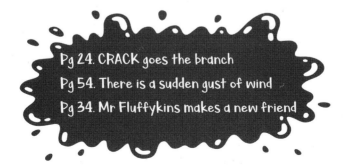

Pg 24. CRACK goes the branch

Pg 54. There is a sudden gust of wind

Pg 34. Mr Fluffykins makes a new friend

To say that Mr Fluffykins is **wrapped** around my head might be a **BIT OF A FIB**. He is more doing **FRANTIC LAPS** around my head. His **sharp, razor-like claws** are sinking into every piece of available flesh as he tries to hang on.

The **spooked cat SPUN** around my head like a **MINI-TORNADO.**

When I finally get back to Mum, all she says is, 'I **think** we **might** need to get you to the **EMERGENCY ROOM . . .**'

Then a **FUNNY THING** happened . . .

Pg 178. Amazing ambulance antics

Pg 8. Just call me Bandaid Boy

The paramedics arrive quickly to treat the wounds caused by Mr Fluffykins.

'Did the big bad pussycat scratch you?' says one with a **snigger**.

The other hands me a lollipop. 'There, there. This will take your mind off the SCARY PUSS-PUSS.'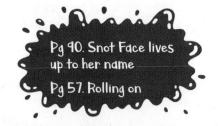

Luckily, my embarrassment is hidden by the mummy-like bandages they wrap around my head. I'm loaded onto a stretcher and shoved into the back of the ambulance.

'We'd better take him to the emergency room to **dip his head in antiseptic**,' the SNIGGERER tells Mum.

Mum and my little sister, **SNOT FACE**, join me in the back of the ambulance.

Then a FUNNY THING happened . . .

Pg 90. Snot Face lives up to her name

Pg 57. Rolling on

179

REALLY?!? Are you crazy? Simon Sidebottom would **NEVER** give up his **final day of holidays** without a **FIGHT!**

Wow, maybe you really **shouLdn't** be reading this book . . .

Go back to **page 7** and MAKE A BETTER CHOICE!

So the **good news** is that I manage to avoid getting **POOPED** on by the giant bird. **GIANT BIRD = GIANT POOP**. That would have been a **revolting mess.**

The bad news is that I am falling a LONG, LONG WAY out of the sky.

The ground is coming up quickly and I can see rooftops looming.

BANG!

I **CRASH** through the roof of a building and come to rest in a sitting position. In fact, I'm resting in quite a comfortable chair. I'm alive and my limbs and internal organs seem to be where they should be. **It's my lucky day!**

Through the **DUST** and **RUBBLE**, I can make out a couple of figures. **They move closer.**

'Oh you must be Simon Sidebottom,' one of the figures says.

182

'You're right on time,' says the other.

The figures **cackle menacingly** and start moving towards me. 'These will only hurt for the **FIRST SIX MONTHS**,'

The dust clears and I can now see where I've fallen.

PINCH AND
BLISTER SHOES!

NOOOOO!

THE END

BANG!

I look up with a **mouthful of dirt and grass**. Mum is closing in quickly. She is a **V–A–M– VERY ANGRY MUM**. Her high-pitched, **angry shriek** sends the neighbourhood's dogs into a HOWLING FRENZY.

'SIMON!

DON'T YOU EVEN THINK OF TRYING TO RUN!'

bellows Mum.

I'm not thinking of running. **I am running**. Coughing up chunks of lawn, I stumble across the yard. I am so very close to my bike. I reach out my fingers, almost touching it when— **WHACK! SNOT FACE**'s Baby Go Potty doll hits the back of my head. Mum's aim is **DEADLY**.

I know when I'm beaten. There's no point in trying to escape.

Then a FUNNY THING happened . . .

Pg 180. Simon gets in the car like a good boy

'Really, REALLY lame,' the stranger continues. 'But I have to give you full points for **SETTING YOUR SNEAKERS ON FIRE**. Let me introduce myself,' the stranger says, taking off their helmet. 'I'm Emma Blister.'

'Any chance you can teach me how to do **eight somersaults?**' I squeak. 'By the way, I'm Simon Sidebottom.' My voice is weirdly high-pitched from the **BIKE VERSUS GROIN MEETING.**

'Sure thing, **Smoking Simon**,' Emma teases. 'But first, I reckon I need to lend you some DECENT SHOES.' She points at my naked toes. 'Follow me.'

Then a FUNNY THING happened . . .

Pg 66. The old man

POP

SNOT FACE is Laughing crazily, thinking that blowing **SNOT BUBBLES** is the funniest thing in the world. Problem is that my little sister laughs so hard that she lets out a **LITTLE WEE**. And by a '**LITTLE WEE**' I mean a lot.

'Great,' exclaims Mum. 'Now I'm going to have to turn the car around and go home and get her changed.'

As we pull into the driveway we hear A COMMOTION.

Then a FUNNY THING happened . . .

Pg 172. Mrs Nesbitt calls for help